Hello, Family Members,

Learning to read is one of the most important accomplishments of early childhood. **Hello Reader!** books are designed to help children become skilled readers who like to read. Beginning readers learn to read by remembering frequently used words like "the," "is," and "and"; by using phonics skills to decode new words; and by interpreting picture and text clues. These books provide both the stories children enjoy and the structure they need to read fluently and independently. Here are suggestions for helping your child *before*, *during*, and *after* reading:

Before

- Look at the cover and pictures and have your child predict what the story is about.
- Read the story to your child.
- Encourage your child to chime in with familiar words and phrases.
- Echo read with your child by reading a line first and having your child read it after you do.

During

- Have your child think about a word he or she does not recognize right away. Provide hints such as "Let's see if we know the sounds" and "Have we read other words like this one?"
- Encourage your child to use phonics skills to sound out new words.
- Provide the word for your child when more assistance is needed so that he or she does not struggle and the experience of reading with you is a positive one.
- Encourage your child to have fun by reading with a lot of expression . . . like an actor!

After

- Have your child keep lists of interesting and favorite words.
- Encourage your child to read the books over and over again. Have him or her read to brothers, sisters, grandparents, and even teddy bears. Repeated readings develop confidence in young readers.
- Talk about the stories. Ask and answer questions. Share ideas about the funniest and most interesting characters and events in the stories.

I do hope that you and your child enjoy this book.

> —Francie Alexander
> Reading Specialist,
> Scholastic's Learning Ventures

For my husband, Charles, who dares me to do my best.
—K.K.

For Stevie
—B.D.

**Go to www.scholastic.com for Web site information
on Scholastic authors and illustrators.**

Text copyright © 2001 by Kathleen Keeler.
Illustrations copyright © 2001 by Bob Doucet.
All rights reserved. Published by Scholastic Inc.
SCHOLASTIC, HELLO READER, CARTWHEEL BOOKS, and associated logos
are trademarks and/or registered trademarks of Scholastic Inc.
ISBN 0-439-32255-3

Library of Congress Cataloging-in-Publication Data

Keeler, Kathleen.
  I double dare you! : more stories to scare you! / by Kathleen Keeler ;
  illustrated by Bob Doucet.
      p. cm. — (Hello reader! Level 3)
"Cartwheel books."
Summary: A collection of three scary stories, all set on Halloween night.
  ISBN 0-439-32255-3 (pbk.)
      1. Halloween—Juvenile fiction. 2. Horror tales, American. 3. Children's stories,
American. [1. halloween—Fiction. 2. Horror stories. 3. Short stories.] I. Doucet, Bob, ill.
II. Title. III. Series.
PZ7.K2265 Iae 2001
[E]—dc21   2001020758

12 11 10 9 8 7 6 5 4 3 2 1   01 02 03 04 05

Printed in the U.S.A.   24
First printing, October 2001

I DOUBLE DARE YOU

More Stories to Scare You

by Kathleen Keeler
Illustrated by Bob Doucet

Hello Reader! — Level 3

SCHOLASTIC INC.

New York   Toronto   London   Auckland   Sydney
Mexico City   New Delhi   Hong Kong

Which Witch Is Which?

It was Halloween night.
Winnie loved her witch costume.
She wore a creepy, black dress.
She wore a pointy, black hat.
She had a long, green nose
with lots of hairy witch warts.
It was horrible.
It was perfect!
Winnie couldn't wait for
everyone to see her.

She grabbed her trick-or-treat bag.
She ran outside.
There was a witch by the tree.
There was a witch by the stop sign.
There was a witch by the mailbox.
There were witches everywhere.

Winnie walked up to the first house.
Ding-dong.
A tall witch gave Winnie some candy.
Ding-dong.
A skinny witch gave Winnie some candy.
Ding-dong.
A fat witch gave Winnie some candy.
There were too many witches!
Winnie did not want to see
any more witches.
But she did want more candy.
She would go just a little farther.

Winnie went down a dark alley.
She had never been there before.
Ding-dong.
Another witch opened the door.
This witch had long, black fingernails.
This witch had cobwebs hanging
from her hat.
This witch had spiders in her hair.
This witch was very spooky.
"Hello, Winnie," the witch cackled.
How did this witch know her name?
"Here is your favorite candy, Wiggle
Wormies."

How did this witch know her favorite candy?

"Say 'hi' to Walt for me," the witch said.

How did this witch know about her baby brother?

Walt wasn't even there.
Eeeeek!
This witch must be a real witch!
Winnie had to get away.

She started running through
the dark.
"Don't forget your math homework,"
the witch called after her.
Eeeeek! This witch must be . . .
her teacher.
How scary!

You made it through the first
story? My, my—very good.
But can you read the next story?
It is even scarier. Do you dare?
Do you double dare?

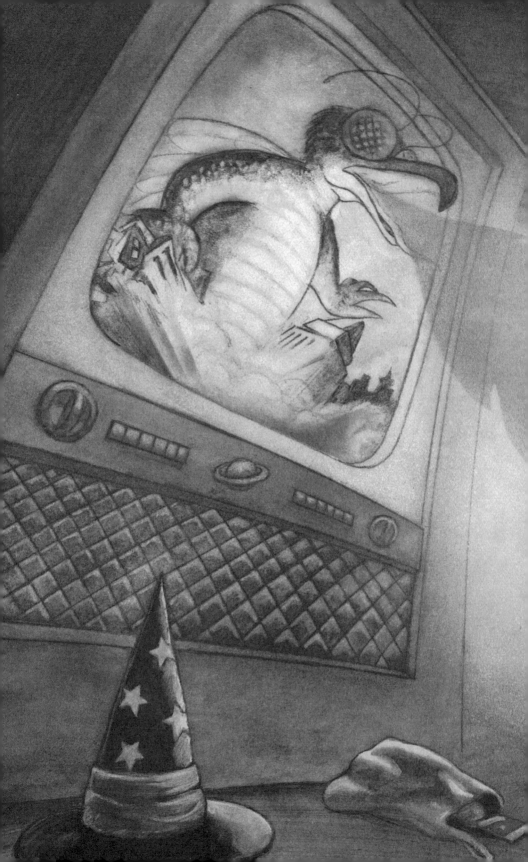

A Monster Tale

It was Halloween night.
Sara snuck downstairs in the dark.
She watched a monster movie.
Sometimes she hid her eyes.
It was too scary.
Sara turned off the TV.
She ran up to her room.
The stairs creaked.
Her door squeaked.

Sara jumped into bed.
She tried to go to sleep.
Scritch-scritch-scratch.

Sara heard something.
She pulled the covers up to her chin.
Scritch-scritch-scratch.
Sara heard it again.
She pulled the covers up to her nose.
Scritch-scritch-scratch.
Sara saw the curtains move.
Something was over there!
Sara pulled the covers over her head.

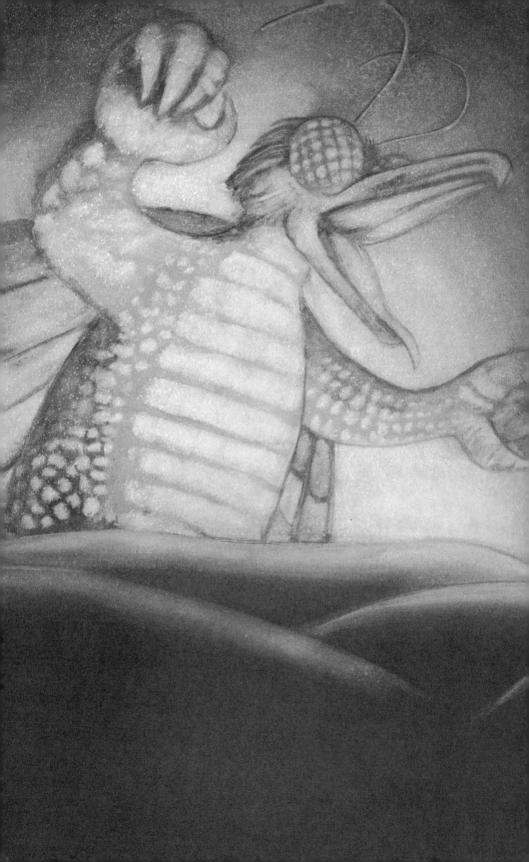

Scritch-scritch-scratch.
Something was coming closer.
Something with scritchy-scratchy claws.
Scritch-scritch-scratch.
Something was moving across her bed.
Something with scritchy-scratchy claws.
What was it?
The monster in the movie had claws.
Big claws.
Long claws.
Sharp claws!

Sara couldn't stand it anymore.
She threw back the covers.
She touched something.
She grabbed it.
Sara could not let go.
She was too scared.
It was twitching.
It was scaly.
It was small.
The monster in the movie had
a twitchy, scaly, small tail.
She must have pulled off
a real monster's tail!
Ahhhhhh!

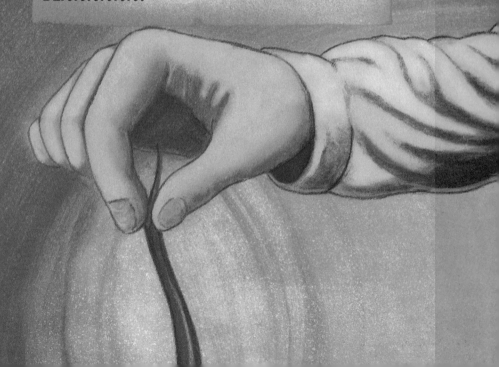

Sara ran down the dark hall.
The monster's tail kept twitching.
"Look! A monster's tail!" Sara screamed.
Mom turned on the light.
Mom looked.
"Not a monster . . . a mouse!" Mom said.
"*Eeee-yuck*," Sara said.
Sara dropped the mouse on the bed.
"*Ahhhhhhhhhhhhhhhhhh!*" Dad screamed.
He hated mice more than monsters!

A Bark in the Dark

It was Halloween night.
"Come on, Elroy," Dave called
to his dog.
Elroy did not come.
Elroy did not want to go trick-or-
treating.

Dogs never got any treats
on Halloween.
Elroy hid under the bed.
Dave found him.
Dave got the leash.
No fair, Elroy thought.

"It's okay, boy," Dave said.
"We're not going trick-or-treating."
Really? Elroy was glad to hear it.
Elroy took off.
He pulled Dave out the door.
He pulled Dave down the street.
"No, Elroy, we aren't going
to the playground."

Drat! Elroy thought.

Elroy took off again.

"No, Elroy, we aren't going to the store."

Rats! Elroy thought.

Elroy took off again.

"No, Elroy, we aren't going to the park."

Cats!!! Elroy smelled them.
He pulled on his leash.
"No, Elroy!" Dave shouted.
Dave held on tight.
"We are not chasing cats!"

Double rats! No cats, thought Elroy.
"We are going to the spooky house,"
Dave explained. "I have to get
a number off of the old mailbox.
It's a Halloween dare."

Dave and Elroy walked up the hill.
They came to the empty house.
There were no street lights.
There was no moon.
There was . . . a black cat.
Yeowl!
Grrrrrr!

Elroy jerked hard.
Dave dropped the leash.
Elroy ran up the walk.
"No!" Dave shouted at Elroy.
Elroy cut through the weeds.
"No!" Dave screamed.
Elroy disappeared into the blackness.

"Oh, no!" Dave shivered. "Elroy," he whispered.

Silence.

"El-rrroy," Dave stuttered.

Yelp! Dave heard his dog bark.

CRASH!

What was that?

Dave took off.

Something was following him.
BANG! BANG! BANG!
Something was catching up with him.
BANG! BANG! BANG!
Something was right next to him.
Dave tripped.
"Ahhhhh!"
Dave fell down.

He felt something hot on his face.
He felt something wet on his face.
He felt something sticky on his face.
What was it?
Blood?
No, it was slobber.
Elroy was licking his face.
"Yuck, Elroy." Dave pushed him away.
Then he saw something was caught
in Elroy's leash.

That was what had been banging!
It was square.
It was metal.
It had rusty numbers on it.
Dave knew just what it was.
"Good dog, Elroy!"
Dave gave Elroy a big kiss.
Yuck! He slobbered on me,
Elroy thought.

"Wait till everyone sees I've got the whole mailbox," Dave said. "We pulled off the best Halloween dare ever!"

I know that last story scared you, right? No? You are very brave. Brave enough . . . to go outside on the darkest Halloween night?